CONTENTS

*Billy Weasel put Harvey's shoe in the water tub to see
if it would float like a boat.*

TEN PAST TWO

It wasn't much fun sitting beside Billy Weasel in Crack Willow Wood School.

On Monday he stole little Harvey Stoat's lunch and ate every bit of it. On Tuesday he sharpened Harvey's new pencil at both ends, and this was a thing Harvey never did with his pencils, he only sharpened them at one end. On Wednesday Billy Weasel put Harvey's shoe in the water tub to see if it would float like a boat.

The shoe filled up with water, and sank.

"Look at that shoe!" said Miss Findlay. "It looks like a ship at the bottom of the sea. How can you be so careless with your things, Harvey Stoat?"

Harvey tried to tell her that Billy Weasel had put the shoe in the water, but Miss Findlay hadn't time to listen. His foot was still wet when he got home, so his mother had something to say, too.

"How did that happen?" said Mrs Stoat. "What were you doing with that foot to get it soaking wet like that?"

"Billy Weasel did it and I don't like school any more and I'm not going back," said Harvey.

He spoke quite loudly. Mr and Mrs Stoat could see that Harvey meant what he said.

"Everybody goes to school," said Mr Stoat. "Your friends Hog and Charity go to school. Every word you learn there is like money in the bank, so let us have no more nonsense and silly talk, Young Stoat. Of course you must go to school."

Harvey wasn't happy. As he lay in bed that night the village clock chimed seven times in the distance. "How lovely it would be," he said to himself, "if the time was always seven o'clock. Then I wouldn't have to go to school any more and I wouldn't have to sit beside Billy Weasel."

When the morning came, Harvey brought a rope to school with him. Everyone asked him what the rope was for, but he wouldn't tell them.

"Are you going to climb a mountain?" asked Hog.

"Are you going to play skipping?" asked Charity Rabbit, who was a very fine skipper.

"He's going to tie up Miss Findlay!" laughed Billy Weasel.

I would like to tie you up, Harvey thought as he glared at Billy Weasel. Instead he added

9

mysteriously, "Wait until ten past two. Then you will see what I am going to do with this rope."

When the village clock struck two, Miss Findlay said goodbye to her class and sent them all home.

At five minutes past two, Harvey climbed up the tower to the village clock with the rope around his shoulders. His friends were amazed to see this happen.

"What is he doing up there?" asked Olivia Vole. The sky was so bright above that she could not see clearly.

"He's unwinding the rope," said Badger. "By Jove, I do believe he's tying up the clock!"

This was a good guess. Far above all their heads, Harvey tied the big hand of the clock to the small one. Now he wound the rope two times around the tower so that the hands

Harvey wound the rope two times around the tower so that the hand could never move.

could never move. Then he came down again.

"You've stopped the village clock!" said Olivia Vole. "That is the most important clock in the world. How will we know what time it is?"

"Everybody will know what time it is," said Harvey. "It will always be ten past two in the afternoon."

No one knew what to think about this, so there was a long silence. Badger looked at Hog, and Hog looked at Charity Rabbit, who said, "But what about school? If it's always ten past two there can't be any school."

"I know," said Harvey. "They'll have to close it down."

Almost everyone who was there that day could see what a wonderful thing Harvey Stoat had just done. No more school! He had turned every day into a holiday. Billy

Weasel was so pleased that he ate his jotter – a thing he had always wanted to do.

Bedtime arrived. Harvey said that he wasn't going to bed because it was still only ten past two in the afternoon. "I tied up the clock with my rope," he explained. "That's how I know what time it is."

Mrs Stoat hurried Harvey into his pyjamas. "I never heard anything so silly," she said to him crossly. "No bedtime, indeed! Look how it's getting dark outside. You can't stop the sun going down at night or coming up in the morning no matter how many clocks you tie up. And you might have fallen down that great big tower and broken your silly leg."

In the morning, Harvey Stoat set off for school with his friends, as usual.

"That was a good idea you had yesterday,

Stoaty," said Hog. "It's a pity it didn't work."

"Oh, I don't know," said Charity Rabbit. "I quite like school."

That's because you don't sit beside Billy Weasel, thought Harvey.

Before long Miss Findlay asked them to set out their jotters on the table for some work with numbers. Everyone did so except for Billy Weasel.

"And where is *your* jotter?" Miss Findlay asked him.

"Billy Weasel ate his jotter yesterday, Miss," said Hog.

"He ate his jotter? He ate his good jotter? How much of it did he eat?"

"All of it," Badger called out.

There was quite a bit of laughing at that, but Billy Weasel didn't think it was funny when Miss Findlay made him sit on his own at the Silly Table.

"And you will sit there until you learn that jotters are not to be eaten like sweets!" she cried.

Harvey felt a little sorry for Billy Weasel, sitting over at the Silly Table without a friend close by. Then he remembered his wet shoe, and did his very best writing with a new pencil sharpened only at one end.

"I'm not inviting Billy Weasel because he's not my friend."

HARVEY'S PARTY

Little Harvey Stoat was buying balloons at the village shop in Crack Willow Wood. It would be his birthday soon, and he was planning to have a barbecue in the back garden. There would be lots to eat, including pizza pieces and sausages on sticks.

"You'll need some invitation cards," said his mum. "Five of them should do."

"I only need four cards," said Harvey. "One for Badger and one for Olivia Vole and one for Hog and one for Charity Rabbit. I'm not inviting Billy Weasel because he's not my friend."

But Mrs Stoat bought five cards. "It wouldn't be nice to invite your other friends and not Billy," she said.

On the way home from the shop, Harvey thought about Billy Weasel. Only that afternoon he'd thrown Harvey's cap up on the school roof. Then he'd laughed when Miss Findlay came along and all Harvey's friends got into trouble for trying to get it down again. Billy Weasel was a rough sort who loved to shout and fight, and he could easily spoil a birthday party.

Harvey went out to play. Down in the woods his friends were playing a game called Custard Bun.

"Hurry up there, Stoaty," called Hog, "we're just about to start. When I shout 'Go' you have to run, and the last one home's a Custard Bun!"

Hog shouted "Go", and everyone made a dash for the big crack willow tree, because the big tree was "home" and the last one to get there was the Custard Bun.

Billy Weasel was so determined to win that he got in everybody's way. He tripped up Olivia Vole, who swerved into Charity Rabbit, who bumped into Badger, who shoved Harvey into a puddle of mud, and Harvey came last.

Everyone pointed at Harvey, and cried, "Custard Bun!"

Harvey didn't mind at all, for this was the point of the game. But, as usual, Billy Weasel went too far.

"Yaa haa, I won, Stoaty is the Custard Bun," he cried in a singsong voice. "Stoaty's made of custard, eat him up with mustard."

This went on for so long that Harvey became quite angry. *I'd like to make you eat mustard*, he thought. It was clear to him now that Billy Weasel was far too silly to come to the party. He would want the biggest piece of cake. He would eat the fattest sausages. Probably, he would laugh out loud if Harvey didn't manage to blow out all his candles at one go.

After tea Harvey wrote out his invitation cards.

"Well," said Mrs Stoat, "have you invited all your friends to the party?"

"Yes, I have," said Harvey. He didn't let his mum see that there was one card left over.

The invitations arrived. Olivia Vole wrote back, saying, "Delighted." Charity Rabbit wrote back saying, "I can't wait!" Badger wrote back saying, "I, Badger, shall be there." And Hog wrote back saying, "I gratefully accept this kind invitation. Your

Humble Servant, Hog."

As for Billy Weasel, he waited patiently for his invitation to the party, but it never came.

On the day of the party, many delicious smells filled Harvey Stoat's back garden. The guests played some birthday games and sang "Happy Birthday to You" as Charity Rabbit played on her fiddle. Then they cheered as Harvey blew out all his candles with one long puff.

Mrs Stoat brought out a jug of lemon drink.

"I wonder why Billy Weasel didn't come. Perhaps he isn't feeling well today. Call me if you need more of anything," she said as she went back into the house.

Just as Harvey had sliced his cake into five pieces, the garden gate burst wide open.

Was this a sudden rush of mighty wind through the forest?

No. Billy Weasel was standing there, and anyone could tell that he was ready for a fight.

"Aha! So *this* is where the lovely smells are coming from?" he cried. "Well, isn't this cosy. Remember me?"

Badger looked at Charity Rabbit, and Charity looked at Olivia Vole, who had just been telling some good jokes to Hog. Harvey Stoat didn't know what to do or where to look.

"Why wasn't I invited?" shouted Billy Weasel. "And I'll have a bit of that cake for a start, Stoaty – the BIGGEST bit!"

This was Billy Weasel at his very worst: full of bad temper and full of bad manners. Poor Harvey thought that his party was about to be ruined. And his mum was sure

"Why wasn't I invited?" shouted Billy Weasel.

to find out that he hadn't sent an invitation to Billy Weasel.

Then Hog stood up and began to speak.

"Well, the party is over, everyone. We've had our fun. And now ... *the last one home's a Custard Bun!*"

Away ran Billy Weasel, running fit to burst. He was determined not to be the last one home to the big crack willow tree in the woods. No one was going to point at him and say, "Billy Weasel's made of custard, eat him up with mustard."

In no more time than it takes to say, he was only a tiny moving dot on the far hill.

Badger and Olivia Vole and Charity Rabbit and Hog finished their birthday cake, and then it was time to go home. They thanked Harvey very much for a fine party, and Harvey gave each of them a party bag to take away. The party bags contained some

fruit and wild honey, some black pudding
especially for Badger, a slice of birthday
cake and, of course, a custard bun.

Billy Weasel stuck up both his arms and waved them wildly.

BILLY WEASEL DIDN'T CARE

One morning Miss Findlay said to her class, "I want someone to take an important parcel up to the office. And he or she must be a sensible person; I don't want anyone silly."

Everybody wanted to take the parcel to the office. In the middle of the back row Badger put up a long arm. Hog tried to make himself look as big as Badger, but found that it was impossible. Charity Rabbit wiggled her ears intelligently to draw attention to herself, and Billy Weasel stuck up both his arms and waved them wildly.

"I'm a sensible person!" he shouted.

"You're not a bit sensible!" Olivia Vole

told him loudly.

"I'm good at carrying parcels," said Harvey Stoat.

"I'm very good at carrying parcels," cried Hog.

"I'm an EXCELLENT parcel-carrier!" boomed Badger.

Miss Findlay decided that Charity Rabbit should take the important parcel to the office. Although Charity had never been in charge of a parcel before, she was sure that she could do it quite well.

"It's a very heavy parcel," she said.

"Then perhaps I should send someone with you," said Miss Findlay.

"Me! I'll help her!" cried Billy Weasel.

"All right," said Miss Findlay. "Both of you can take the parcel. And remember that I expect you to behave yourselves when you are out of this classroom. This is your chance to show how good you can be, Billy Weasel."

Charity Rabbit and Billy Weasel set off together. Charity carried the important parcel and Billy Weasel led the way. At the end of the corridor they saw a door that was partly open.

"Come on," whispered Billy Weasel, "I want to show you something."

"But that isn't the office."

"Don't be such a scaredy-cat," said Billy Weasel, and he went right in.

Charity peeped round the door to see what he was up to. Billy Weasel was wearing a cap that was miles too big for him. Also, he had picked up the patrol lady's Lollipop – the one that stopped all the traffic on the main road.

"*Brrrm, brrrm, vroooom,*" said Billy Weasel. "I am in charge of this Lollipop.

STOP!" And he held out his arm as if Charity was a great big truck thundering down the road.

"What are you two doing in here?" said a cross voice.

It was the patrol lady! She had caught them in her room. Charity stared at the ground, but Billy Weasel didn't care.

"We are taking an important parcel to the office," he said.

"Are you indeed! Well, this is not the office, so off you go. And give me back my cap!"

They walked on down the corridor. Soon, Billy Weasel decided that walking was too slow. He began to zoom, even though zooming was not allowed inside school. He zoomed down the corridor in zigs and zags until he came to an empty classroom.

This was the Music Room, but Billy

"What are you two doing in here?" said a cross voice.

Weasel didn't care. He went right in.

He tinkled the piano, high notes and low. He tapped the drums and made them go *boom, boom ta-ta boom*. Then he picked up two sticks and began to bash the xylophone.

Charity longed to play something, too. *Maybe*, she thought, *maybe I could just press down on the piano keys and make one little tinkle!*

And she did.

"What are you two doing in here?" said a voice.

It was the violin teacher, and she had caught them in the Music Room! Charity was so ashamed that she wanted to disappear, for she knew that they shouldn't be here at all. But Billy Weasel didn't care.

"We are taking an important parcel to the office," he said.

"Are you indeed! Well, the office does not

32

have a piano, or drums, or a xylophone, so off you go this minute."

They hurried away. This time Charity hoped that Billy Weasel would go straight to the office, but he didn't. When they came to the Assembly Hall, he walked right in.

Lots of things were happening in the Assembly Hall. Some of the class had hoops, others were skipping, or balancing on a beam, or climbing up ropes. Billy Weasel decided that he would like to climb a rope, so he did. He climbed right to the top and laughed at everyone down below.

A teacher on the stage clapped to show that she wanted quiet. "Right, everyone, into your groups. And be ready to change when I count to..."

When I count to three, she was about to say. Then she noticed two bodies in the hall who should not have been there at all.

"You two! What are you doing here? Does your teacher know where you are?"

Of course she doesn't know, thought Charity, who wanted to run away and hide. Miss Findlay would have a fit if she saw them now! But Billy Weasel didn't care.

"We are taking an important parcel to the office," he said.

"Well, you won't find the office up that rope! This is the Assembly Hall, so hurry along, please."

They left the Hall, but Billy Weasel did not hurry. He opened doors and peeped in, and looked at pictures on the walls, and swung upside down on coat-pegs.

"I like taking parcels to the office," he said.

At last they came to the front hall of the school. Here, just inside the main door, there was a large tank full of lovely golden fish. Billy Weasel looked round to make sure that all was quiet. Then he rolled up his sleeve.

"What are you going to do?" Charity asked him, although she had an awful feeling that she knew exactly what he meant to do.

"Catch one. It's my turn to carry the parcel now." To make himself taller and able to reach more easily, Billy Weasel stood on Miss Findlay's important parcel and plunged his arm into the tank.

The fish didn't like him. They swished their tails and darted away, but even so, he almost had one when...

"*Billy Weasel!* What are you doing with those fish?"

Miss Findlay had arrived, and she was so cross that Charity Rabbit didn't dare look at her face. Billy Weasel, caught in the act, jumped into the air, and the drips of water running off him made a messy little puddle beside the parcel on the floor.

"So this is what took you so long! Do you realize that you have been gone for twenty whole minutes? And what are you doing? Actually using my parcel to stand on while you catch fish! Charity, did this rascal show you the way to the office?"

"No, Miss Findlay. He showed me the big Lollipop and the Music Room and he went into the Hall and climbed up a rope."

"A rope!"

Billy Weasel spoke up loudly. "She played the piano, I saw her."

"I only played it once, Billy Weasel!" shouted Charity. "And, Miss Findlay, then he made me look at the fish and he didn't carry the parcel at all, I had to carry it the whole way by myself."

"I see," Miss Findlay said slowly. "Well, the next time I send a note or a parcel to the office, Billy Weasel will not be with you. You can take it by yourself. Now let us go back to our classroom, where I shall have something more to say about this!"

Charity Rabbit walked nicely behind Miss Findlay, but Billy Weasel skipped down the corridor as if he *still* didn't care.

Harvey poked his stick through the holes where the eyes used to be.

THE DEAD-HEAD

Harvey Stoat was playing down by the stream with Olivia Vole when he found an interesting skull. It was just lying there among the nettles and Harvey poked it out with a stick.

Olivia didn't like it. "That dead-head gives me the creeps," she said as Harvey poked his stick through the holes where the eyes used to be. "And I wish you wouldn't do that to its eyes, Stoaty."

The jawbone of the skull still had some teeth. "I think I'll bring this dead-head into school tomorrow," said Harvey.

"It'll be smelly!" Olivia warned him.

"It won't be smelly if I wash it," said Harvey.

As Harvey washed the dead-head that evening, his mother came to peep over his shoulder. "What on earth is that, Harvey Stoat?" she said.

"I found this dead-head and I have to bring it into school. Miss Findlay will want to see its teeth."

"Are you sure?"

"She likes teeth," Harvey explained. "We're learning all about teeth in school and she wants us to bring things in."

"Well, put it in a bag, for goodness' sake. And wash your hands, who knows where that old bone has been!"

On the way to school next morning Harvey felt quite important because he had a bag with a dead-head and fourteen teeth inside it.

Olivia Vole also had a bag with her. Harvey was worried in case this turned out to be another dead-head, because he'd thought of bringing in a dead-head first and therefore Olivia Vole was a copycat if she had one, too. But no. It was only a story-book about teeth.

As soon as Miss Findlay opened up Harvey's bag, everyone was interested in the dead-head. Whose had it been? Where had Harvey found it? Why did it look so clean? Billy Weasel wanted to know where the rest of it was. And how had it died?

"Ooo, the poor thing!" cried Charity Rabbit.

"It really is an interesting skull," said Miss Findlay. "See how the jaws still move. Let's count its teeth."

"Fourteen!" cried Harvey.

"And see how they are worn down. This

tells us that the animal ate grass when it was alive. We'll draw this skull later today, but now, I think I'll read out Olivia's story about teeth. So sit up and listen."

Miss Findlay looked hard at Billy Weasel. Sometimes he talked all the way through stories, and rolled about the floor instead of sitting up properly on the carpet.

The story was about someone with a wobbly tooth. The tooth wobbled so much that it came out, but that was only the beginning of the story. The tooth was put into a glass of water, and then tooth fairies came in the dark of night and flew away with it. And they left money in the glass of water where the tooth used to be.

"Did you like that story?" asked Miss Findlay.

"It was quite good," said Badger.

"It was a lovely story," said Charity Rabbit.

"I think I may have heard something like it before," observed Hog.

"How much money did those fairies leave?" asked Harvey Stoat.

"Oh, it doesn't say," said Miss Findlay. "I should think probably a one pound coin."

Harvey shook his head as if he couldn't believe what he was hearing. A whole one pound coin! Money was one of Harvey Stoat's favourite things, but he could never keep it. The trouble was that you had to spend money in the shops to enjoy it, and then you didn't have it any more. The shopkeeper had it.

That afternoon, when the class made drawings of the dead-head, Miss Findlay's eyes grew round and wide when she saw Harvey's page. He had drawn fourteen little coins instead of fourteen little teeth.

"It's a sort of money-head," Harvey explained.

"And what is this supposed to be?" she asked.

"It's a sort of money-head," Harvey explained.

"Very interesting, but we do not want a money-head, we want a skull with proper teeth, please." And she made him start again.

At home time, everyone was in a good mood coming out of school. Olivia was pleased that her story had been read out and Harvey was pleased that his dead-head had been such a great success.

"I think I'll probably be rich tomorrow," he said to his friends.

"Why is that?" asked Charity Rabbit, but Harvey wouldn't tell her about his wonderful plan for getting money.

When he got home his mother asked him what he had learned in school that day.

"I learned that tooth fairies leave you money if you give them teeth," said Harvey. "I think I might be rich tomorrow."

"Oh? Have you a wobbly tooth?"

"No!" laughed Harvey. His mother didn't understand. He wasn't giving away his own teeth.

That night he took the teeth out of his dead-head and put them into a glass of water. Then he began to wonder, would fourteen one pound coins fit into just one glass? Harvey wasn't sure. He sneaked into the kitchen and got eight more glasses and three cups and two mugs so that each tooth could be on its own. There was just enough room on his bedside table for this grand plan.

As he lay in bed thinking about all the wonderful things that money could buy, Harvey could hardly get to sleep. Not that he minded. It would be exciting to be awake when those tooth fairies came! Probably they would be amazed when they saw so many glasses and so many lovely clean teeth.

When Harvey woke up next morning, all the glasses, cups and mugs were gone from his bedside table, except for one glass lying on his floor in pieces. His mum was down on her knees, brushing up all the dangerous little sparkling bits.

"Ah! So you're awake," said Mrs Stoat.

There were no glasses and there was no money. Something must have gone wrong with his great plan!

"Don't you dare get out of that bed or you'll cut your feet," said Mrs Stoat. "You're lucky only one of my good glasses was broken. All those things on your bedside table! Have you gone mad, Harvey Stoat?"

"I didn't do it," said Harvey.

"Oh? Did it fall off the table by itself?"

"The tooth fairies must have broken it."

"Nonsense, the tooth fairies don't waste their money on a dead-head's teeth. It has to be your own tooth, and you're the one to blame. Do your friends Hog and Badger bring fourteen glasses full of water to bed at night? No!"

On the way to school that morning, Harvey didn't say much to his friends. He didn't say anything at all to Olivia Vole, because if Olivia Vole hadn't brought that book to school he wouldn't be in trouble. He blamed her as well as those stupid tooth fairies.

Miss Findlay called the roll and told them to set out their books. "Today we are going to start with our news," she said.

Good, thought Harvey. There were things

in his head that he wanted to write down. After a little while he put up his hand. "Miss Findlay, can you tell me how to spell 'cheaters'?"

Miss Findlay wrote "cheaters" on the board. "Are you sure that's the word you want?" she asked.

Harvey was very sure about the word he wanted. He'd put a lot of work into those teeth and all they'd done was get him into trouble. He'd even washed them and now he wished that he hadn't washed them.

He wrote:

My mummy shouted at me before I had my breakfast. Those tooth fairies broke one of our good glasses, I got the blame, they didn't leave me any money and they are CHEATERS.

"I'm not feeling happy today, Stoaty," said Badger.

HAPPY TUESDAY, BADGER

Badger woke up one Tuesday feeling down in the dumps. It was a lovely morning. The sun was shining and a warm breeze blew through the trees. This was exactly the kind of day that Badger usually liked so much, but for some reason he didn't feel good. He would have been quite happy to go back to bed and lie there until lunchtime.

"I'm not feeling happy today, Stoaty," he said on the way to school, "and I don't understand why. I haven't got any great worries, you know."

"Maybe it was something you ate for

breakfast," Harvey said helpfully.

"No, I wasn't happy before I had breakfast. I was thinking that maybe I don't like Tuesdays. There was a day last week when I didn't feel happy and I think that was a Tuesday, too."

"I never heard of anybody not liking Tuesdays," said Harvey as they went through the school gates.

The school day began quietly. Charity Rabbit and Olivia Vole talked in whispers about how cross Miss Findlay looked today, and Billy Weasel chased a wasp during roll-call.

"Billy Weasel," said Miss Findlay. "If that wasp doesn't manage to sting you, I certainly will!"

"Badger's not happy with himself today, Miss," said Harvey.

"What's wrong with him?"

"He says he doesn't like Tuesdays."

"Oh, we all have days like that," said Miss Findlay. "Badger will just have to give himself a good shake and he'll feel much better."

But if anything, Badger felt worse as they came home from school. "I'm quite worried, Stoaty," he said. "Maybe I'll feel like this next Tuesday, and every Tuesday for the rest of my life."

"I don't think so," Harvey replied brightly. "We're off school next week, so that Tuesday should be a good one!"

"You may be right," Badger said sadly as he plodded indoors; but he didn't sound too sure.

Harvey could see that something must be done about his friend's problem. But what? How could he show Badger that Tuesdays were just as much fun as

Wednesdays or Thursdays?

A week went by and it was Tuesday again. When Badger looked out of his window he saw all his friends standing there. Each of them had brought along something to make Tuesday interesting.

"Hurry up there, Badger," cried Hog, who carried a sign saying TUESDAYS FOR EVER! "Let's have some fun!"

"A game of Pass the Parcel," said Charity Rabbit, holding up her fiddle.

"And you can have a swing on this," shouted Billy Weasel, showing the rubber tyre he'd found at the edge of the wood.

Badger hurried out to play with his friends. First they took turns at swinging to and fro in the rubber tyre under the great crack willow tree, and then they played Pass the Parcel. Luckily, Charity Rabbit stopped playing her fiddle just when Badger had the

*Each of Badger's friends had brought along something
to make Tuesday interesting.*

last parcel, for it turned out to be three slices of black pudding.

"My favourite, by Jove!" cried Badger. "So far, this has been a very good Tuesday indeed. So far."

They went for a walk along the bank of the river, where Hog spotted something stuck among the water lilies.

"I see a bottle over there. I wonder where it came from."

Olivia Vole, the best swimmer, swam out to bring the bottle back. It looked like a truly ancient bottle. At least a hundred years old, said Hog.

"There's something inside it," cried Charity Rabbit. "I think it might be a note! Ooo! I've always wanted to find a note in a bottle."

Very carefully, Harvey Stoat teased the

crumbly old piece of brown paper from the neck of the bottle. He could just make out the words written on one side:

I buried my treasure in Crack Willow Wood.

I buried my treasure as well as I could.

I buried my treasure as deep as could be In the dark at the top of the crack willow tree.

"Treasure!" said Billy Weasel, as if it was one of those magical words that made all dreams come true. "It's somebody's buried treasure! This could mean silver and gold."

Badger was the best digger.

"And lovely jewels," added Olivia Vole, her own eyes sparkling rather like jewels.

"Only if we can find it. Let us not get ourselves overexcited," Hog warned sensibly, but he was talking to himself. The others were already on their way to the crack willow tree.

They all knew the fine big tree at the edge of Crack Willow Wood. Harvey Stoat and his friends played there all the time. But they faced a mighty problem when they got there.

"It doesn't make any sense," said Badger. "How can you bury treasure in the top of a tree? You just can't."

"Unless 'dark top' means 'shadow'," Charity pointed out. "The treasure might be buried right at the end of the tree's shadow, just over there."

"I say, very good thinking," said Hog, who sounded impressed. "The shadow marks the spot. Let's get digging!"

Badger was the best digger. The soil soon began to fly once he got started. After a while he stopped, and said, "By Jove!" very quietly, for there was a long brown box at the bottom of the hole he'd just dug.

"I'm so excited," cried Charity Rabbit, "what can this be!"

"It's that fellow's treasure," said Hog. "Quick, Badger, open the box and see!"

When Badger opened the box he found a strange kind of treasure in there. It was a long black pudding with HAPPY TUESDAY, BADGER written along it. A whole black pudding!

"Fooled you, fooled you!" shouted Billy Weasel.

Now Charity Rabbit lifted up her fiddle, and began to play. And as she played, everyone sang out as loudly as they could:

"Happy Tuesday to you,
Happy Tuesday to you,
Happy Tuesday, dear Badger,
Happy Tuesday to you."

"Thank you," said Badger. "Thank you very much. I don't think I will ever complain about Tuesdays again – not when I have so many wonderful friends."

It was getting late in Crack Willow Wood. The high trees were dark against the sky already, and Olly Owl would be on the prowl soon. A voice in the distance called someone in for bed. Charity Rabbit, Billy Weasel, Hog, Olivia Vole, Badger and Harvey Stoat walked home together towards the village.

They were looking forward to Wednesday.

THE

END

MORE WALKER STORYBOOKS
For You to Enjoy

Name   _____

Address   _____

_____

J 106, 209   £ 3.99.

First published in Great Britain in 1999 by
Macdonald Young Books

Reprinted in 2000 by Hodder Wayland,
an imprint of Hodder Children's Books

Hodder Children's Books
A division of Hodder Headline
338 Euston Road
London NW1 3BH

Designed and Typeset by Don Martin
Printed in Hong Kong by Wing King Tong Co. Ltd.

British Library Cataloguing in Publication Data available

ISBN: 0 7500 2678 2 (pb)

TESSA POTTER

THE GHOSTS OF
GOLFHAWK SCHOOL

Illustrated by Gillian Hunt

HODDER
Wayland

an imprint of Hodder Children's Books